GHOST
DOG

Read all the books about Barkley's School for Dogs!

Coming Soon!

GHOST DOG

By Marcia Thornton Jones and Debbie Dadey

Illustrated by Amy Wummer

SCHOLASTIC INC.

New York Toronto London Auckland Sydney
Mexico City New Delhi Hong Kong Buenos Aires

To our new puppy Skip, who is white just like a
ghost!—DD

For Judy Minnehan, Lewanna Sexton, Lee
Bamberger, and Julie Bomar—MTJ

ISBN 0-439-37987-3

12 11 10 9 8 7 6 5 4 3 2 1   2 3 4 5 6 7/0

Printed in the U.S.A.   40

First Scholastic printing, January 2002

This book is set in 14-point Cheltenham.

Book design by Dawn Adelman

Contents

WITHOUT A TRACE

"Where is it?" Sweetcakes snarled, showing one yellow fang.

"Where, where," Clyde panted, from his usual spot behind Sweetcakes.

I didn't know what Sweetcakes was looking for, but there was no use trying to answer. Sweetcakes isn't the kind of dog you'd call a good listener. It's a Fido Fact that she's the meanest Doberman pinscher this side of Denver.

I'm Jack, and I'm no pushover, but Sweetcakes is mean enough to get any dog

worried. "What did you lose?" I asked. I looked around Barkley's School for Dogs play yard.

Sweetcakes growled. "Give me back my bone. I know you have it."

"Yeah, yeah," Clyde said.

Sweetcakes kept an old red bone for chewing and didn't let anyone else near it. She was ready for a fight, but I was going to disappoint her. I didn't have her bone.

"Look, Sweetcakes," I said as nicely as I could. "I haven't seen your bone for days. Maybe it's in the same place as my toy." My toy had been snatched yesterday. I had no proof, but I figured Sweetcakes had taken it. That's just the kind of thing Sweetcakes would do. Sweetcakes's name went with her about as well as a bikini goes with a polar bear.

My good friends Floyd, Blondie, and Woodrow came running over to see what Sweetcakes was barking about.

Floyd was a beagle and he did what beagles do best: fetched. Today he had a brand-new leather ball in his mouth.

"Somebody stole my bone," Sweetcakes snapped at Floyd. "Maybe it was you?"

Floyd backed up so fast he bumped into Woodrow.

Woodrow's ears almost dragged on the ground as he stepped around Floyd.

Woodrow didn't bat an eye when his oversized black nose sniffed the ground at Sweetcakes's paws. Being a basset hound, Woodrow never hurried anywhere, but he made up for his lack of speed in the brains department. If anybody bothered to ask me, I'd be the first to say that Woodrow had more smarts than any dog in the yard. He's also the best friend a dog could have.

"Come to think of it," Woodrow said in his slow, deep voice, "strange things have been happening lately here at Barkley's School."

Barkley's School for Dogs was my home away from home. Every morning, my human, Maggie, dropped me off on her way to school. Things were never exactly normal at Barkley's, but I wasn't sure what Woodrow meant.

Blondie used a paw to brush soft white hair from her eyes. She's the most beautiful dog I've ever set my brown eyes on. Her poodle-white hair floated around her like a halo. "Woodrow is right. Just this morning my favorite brush vanished," she said, "without a trace."

"Just like my toy," I added.

"And my bone," Sweetcakes growled.

Woodrow yawned and snuggled into his favorite pile of rags. "Very mysterious," he said before closing his eyes. "All of them disappeared without a trace. Sounds like the work of a ghost, to me."

Floyd dropped the ball he'd been chewing. "Dog-awesome!" he howled. "Barkley's School for Dogs has a ghost!"

GHOSTLY LEGEND

"That's the craziest thing I've ever heard," I snapped. After all, I tend to think of myself as Jack, the Wonder Dog; and a Wonder Dog certainly wouldn't believe in ghosts.

Woodrow opened one eye. "Not so silly," he said, "considering the legend of Rusty."

"Legend?" I asked. I hoped nobody noticed how my voice squeaked just a little.

Blondie shivered and nudged one of Woodrow's ears. "Tell us the legend," she said.

Woodrow opened his other eye and yawned. Dogs wandered in from all over the yard to listen. Two Irish setters plopped beside Blondie, and a Chihuahua snuggled under one of Woodrow's rags. A puppy named Bubba licked my nose and leaned against me. Even Sweetcakes and Clyde sat down to hear the legend. Floyd plopped onto the ground and chewed his leather ball while Woodrow started the story.

"Many years ago a settler decided to carve out a life in the wilderness with his faithful dog, Rusty."

"All dogs are faithful," I said.

"Shhh," Blondie said with a nudge to my shoulder. "Let Woodrow tell it."

"It was back in the olden days," Woodrow said. "Before speeding cars and tall buildings. Back then, this area was covered by so many trees it would take a dog a year just to sniff half of them."

"Did lots of people live here then?" Bubba, the puppy, asked.

Woodrow shook his head. "The settler had no human friends. People thought he was strange for wanting to live in the forest. If they'd taken the time to know him, they would've known that he just liked being in the wilderness with beavers and chipmunks, birds and squirrels, foxes and deer," Woodrow continued. "For nearly a year the settler and his dog, Rusty, roamed the forest."

My tail thumped on the ground as if it had a mind of its own. "Wow," I said. "Think of the fun Maggie and I would have wandering from tree to tree. It sounds like the perfect life!"

"Not so perfect," Woodrow warned. "The most fearsome animal in the forest was the bear. One day a bear attacked the settler. Since he had no friends, nobody was there to help him. Rusty, being the loyal and brave dog that he was, came to the rescue. There was a terrible fight, and Rusty died."

"Poor Rusty," Blondie said.

"The settler was so sad he moved back East," Woodrow said. "He couldn't stand to live in the forest without his dog."

I sat up tall and puffed out my chest. "Everyone knows dogs are loyal," I said. "I'd do the same for my human, Maggie."

Woodrow's ears dragged along the

ground when he nodded. "This dog was more loyal than most," he said. "Long after Rusty died, people said a ghost dog could be seen wandering through the forest. They say it was Rusty, back from the dead, searching for his human."

Sweetcakes stood up and sneered. "What does that have to do with my bone?"

Woodrow scratched one of his long floppy ears before answering. "That settler lived on this very spot. Maybe, just maybe, our missing items are the work of Rusty, the ghost dog!"

"That's all a bunch of doggy drool," Sweetcakes muttered.

"Drool," Clyde said.

"Excuse me," Bubba said in a trembling voice. "I didn't want to say anything before, but this morning I saw something white slink across the yard."

I knew Bubba was a sensible pup, so

his words bothered me. A lot. I looked around the yard where we stood. Barkley's play yard was filled with brightly colored tunnels, jumping bars, and even a seesaw. Let me tell you, I don't scare easily, but hearing what Bubba had to say made the hair on the back of my neck bristle. I had the strange feeling that someone—or something—was watching me.

I worried it might just be a ghost dog.

TRAP

"You pups are crazy," Sweetcakes growled and stomped away.

Clyde ran after her muttering, "Crazy, crazy."

Bubba curled up next to Woodrow. He looked worried.

Floyd stopped chewing his ball and gave it to Bubba. "Here, chew on this, kid. Chewing makes a dog feel better."

"We all need to stay calm," Blondie said. "These mysterious happenings must have something to do with

14

Sweetcakes. It's just like her to take all our things."

I liked Blondie's idea right away. "That's right," I said. "There are no such things as ghosts. Rusty the ghost is nothing more than a made-up story. Sweetcakes is probably playing a trick on us."

"But what about her bone?" Bubba asked.

Floyd shook his head left and right. "Sweetcakes could've hidden her bone just to trick us."

I nodded. "That sounds like something Sweetcakes would do."

Woodrow put his head back down on his paws. "If that's her plan, then it's working," he said. "I think I need a nap."

"How can you sleep?" Bubba asked. "What if the ghost dog comes while you're napping?"

Bubba's question made me shiver all

the way down to the tip of my tail. Then I got mad. After all, a Wonder Dog isn't supposed to be tricked, and he's definitely not supposed to get scared.

"Sweetcakes and Clyde are only trying to make us squirm," I told Bubba.

Bubba dropped Floyd's ball and looked up at me with his puppy-dog eyes. "Are you sure, Jack?" Bubba asked. "Are you sure there's not a ghost?"

"As sure as a dog can be," I told him, "and I'll prove it to you."

"What are you going to do?" Blondie asked.

I smiled at Blondie. "Don't worry," I told her. "Jack, the Wonder Dog is on the case. I'll set a trap for Sweetcakes and catch her in the act."

4

DROOLING SLOBS

Catching Sweetcakes at her evil game wouldn't be easy, but I, Jack, the Wonder Dog, could do it. Fred Barkley, the owner of Barkley's School for Dogs, had other ideas. He swung open the back door, set down a treat bag, and rang a bell. "Practice time," he yelled.

Fred is the head human at Barkley's School. Every day he makes us practice things like sitting, shaking hands, and rolling over. Sometimes he has us run, jump, and balance on the equipment scattered in the backyard. Fred always gives us treats if we do the trick right.

Dogs of every size, color, and shape raced to Fred. Two golden retrievers leaped over a little white Westie, and Sweetcakes bumped a dog with a bald patch on his rump. Fred had us line up like ducks in an arcade game.

As usual, Sweetcakes went first. She sat up and begged. It made me roll my eyes. How could she act so innocent when she was stealing our things and lying about

it? Let me tell you, it made my blood boil to watch her prance around while the rest of us poor pooches drooled and waited. I couldn't wait to catch her playing a trick on us.

Clyde was next in line. He fell over when Fred asked him to sit up and beg. Blondie had no problem. She sat up like a queen in a royal parade.

I can shake hands like a car salesman, but sitting up and begging is something

I've never mastered. Don't get me wrong,
I gave it a try. Up. *Splat.* Up. *Splat.* I fell
down every time. Fred didn't hold it
against me, though. He gave me a pat on
my head and said, "Good try. You'll do
better next time."

I grinned and watched the rest of the
pooches. Floyd had about as much luck
as I did. Surprisingly, Woodrow sat up and

begged as though he did it every day, instead of napping all the time.

Usually I didn't mind the whole practice thing, just today I had bigger things on my mind.

I wanted to catch Sweetcakes, but like most dogs I lose my cool when treats are mentioned. The very word makes me dance around like a puppy chasing a string. So when Fred said, "Good job, dogs, I think you deserve treats," I was ready. Let me tell you, the tails in the play yard were wagging like crazed windshield wipers.

"Fang-tastic!" Floyd cheered. We all lined up, waiting for those juicy, melt-in-your-mouth treats.

"Oh, no!" Fred yelled. "The treat bag is gone!"

"It's the ghost dog," Floyd whined.

5

WONDER DOG ACTION

You can mess with a dog's brush. You can mess with a dog's toy, but you can't—and I repeat—cannot mess with a dog's treat supply. Missing toys were bad, but a whole bag of treats disappearing was terrible. Things had grown very serious.

There was only one dog in the yard capable of such behavior. Sweetcakes. It had to be her. I sneered at her when she and Clyde walked across the yard.

Something had to be done. It was up to me to catch Sweetcakes and her wicked sidekick, Clyde, with the bag of treats. It was time for true Wonder Dog action.

I waited for Fred to go back inside and for all the other dogs in the yard to settle down. Slowly I crept across the play yard. Nose low. Tail to the ground. Belly dragging. Closer. Closer.

I edged around the seesaw, crawled through a tunnel, crept around a bush. I moved closer to Sweetcakes and Clyde. I was so close I could smell Sweetcakes's bad breath. The two evildoers snoozed on the ground, trying to look innocent. I knew better.

I backed under the bush until I was well hidden, ready to watch until Sweetcakes made her move.

Dogs are experts at lying around, and I'm better at it than most. Waiting was easy. Staying awake takes work. The cool breeze ruffled my fur and swished through the branches of the trees. Brown leaves rustled as they rolled across the yard. The sun warmed my head and made me drowsy.

Eyes open wide. Eyes drooping. Eyes closed. *Pop!* Eyes wide open. Eyes drooping. Eyes closed. *Pop!* I had to stay awake!

It didn't help that Sweetcakes and Clyde started snoring. Clyde even echoed Sweetcakes in his sleep. Sweetcakes would snore, "Snarfrrrrr," and Clyde would echo, "Snarf. Snarf." It would have been funny if I wasn't so sleepy. If

something didn't happen soon, I would be Clyde's snoring echo.

Something did happen, but it wasn't what I expected. Sweetcakes and Clyde were still snoring when a howl pierced the play yard. I knew that voice.

It was my buddy Floyd and something was wrong.

99%

"It's gone!" Floyd wailed. "My ball is gone!"

"Are you sure you didn't leave it somewhere?" I asked, rushing to Floyd's side.

Floyd looked at me like I'd turned purple. "I had it in my mouth for nap time. When I woke up it was gone! Gone, I tell you!"

Bubba bounced around me. "I bet Sweetcakes took it. She probably was mad because her bone was missing."

"The nerve of her," Blondie said. "She's

always been a bully, but this has gone too far."

Floyd whined. "Sweetcakes is mean, mean, *MEAN*."

"Let's not jump to conclusions," Woodrow said slowly. "Did anybody *SEE* Sweetcakes with Floyd's ball?"

Floyd looked at Blondie. Blondie looked at Bubba.

Blondie nodded. "It doesn't matter if we saw her or not. She's guilty and I know it."

"How about you, Jack?" Woodrow asked, looking straight at me. "Did you catch Sweetcakes in the act?"

I looked down at my paws. "I tried to stay awake," I said. "But I guess I dozed off for just a minute."

"See!" Floyd said. "Sweetcakes had plenty of time to sneak over here and grab my ball!"

Now, I'm an honest dog. I knew

Sweetcakes was a little on the mean side, but something about this whole scene didn't seem quite right. After all, the yard at Barkley's School for Dogs was big with plenty of room to run. Could Sweetcakes really have made it all the way over to Floyd during my short little nap? She was fast, but was she that fast? I was ninety-nine percent sure that Sweetcakes was guilty, but I couldn't be one hundred percent sure.

Woodrow asked the question I was thinking. "What if Sweetcakes and Clyde didn't take it?"

Floyd glared at Bubba. "Maybe you took it," Floyd accused Bubba. "I did let you chew on it this morning. Maybe you wanted to keep it for yourself!"

Bubba looked hurt. Then he looked mad. "I didn't take your ball. I'm sorry I even looked for it. Besides, how do we know you didn't just lose it?"

Floyd growled. "I would never lose my favorite toy. After all, I'm a *BEAGLE!* And I wouldn't lose my toy!"

Blondie stepped between Floyd and Bubba. "Let's not start blaming each other. There must be an explanation."

"There's always an explanation for things," Woodrow said. "It just may not be what you expect."

"What's that supposed to mean?" I asked.

Woodrow yawned and circled his bed of rags three times before answering. "I only mean that everyone is convinced it's Sweetcakes. Everyone, that is, except me."

"But Sweetcakes is just the kind of dog to do something low-down like this," Floyd told him.

"Without proof," Woodrow told us, "you cannot blame her. Besides, I am pretty sure Sweetcakes is innocent."

"What?" we all gasped.

"How can you say that?" Blondie asked.

"Because," Woodrow said, "I know for a fact that Jack was watching Sweetcakes, and he would've heard her stir from her napping spot. Let's face it, Clyde can't do anything quietly. If either one had budged from their spot, Jack would've heard them."

I stood up tall and puffed out my chest. Woodrow was right. Even if my eyelids

had gotten a bit heavy, I would've known
if Sweetcakes and Clyde had gotten up.

"But if it's not Sweetcakes, and it's not
one of us, who could it be?" Floyd asked.

"Maybe," Bubba said slowly, "there
really *is* a ghost dog!"

HAUNTED

Long shadows cut across the yard and a cold wind sent leaves scattering. Blondie, Floyd, Woodrow, Bubba, and I huddled behind the shed. We were trying to figure out what to do about our haunted school.

Not a single idea was any good. Clearly, none of us had ever caught a ghost before. Even I had to admit that catching a ghost was not something Wonder Dogs do every day.

"Ghosts are no laughing matter," I told my friends. "If we don't do something, we'll be doomed to spending our days in a haunted school. Since this particular ghost seems to enjoy snatching our stuff, we can say good-bye to treats and toys forever."

"If I ever catch up with that ghost dog, I'll knock him out of this yard," Floyd told me, "but only after I get back my ball."

"You'd have to catch him first," Bubba pointed out. "I'm pretty sure a ghost isn't something you can sink your teeth into and fetch."

"We have to get him," Floyd said. "That was a brand-new ball. My human gave it to me for my birthday. I want it back."

I nodded. Gifts from humans were special. I would be brokenhearted if a ghost snatched one of Maggie's gifts to me.

Woodrow slowly shook his head. "A ghost isn't something you can catch," he said.

"Then we'll have to trick the ghost into leaving," I said. "First, we have to find him."

"How do you find something you can't see?" Bubba asked.

The pup had a point. Finding a ghost was like looking for air or wind. You knew it was there but you couldn't see it. "Maybe we should try thinking like a ghost," I suggested.

"Exactly how does a ghost think?" Blondie asked.

I shrugged. "Can you think of a better idea?"

"I'll try it," Bubba said. He closed his eyes and slunk across the yard.

"AROOOOOO! I am a ghost dog," he howled. "AROOOOOO!"

I had to admit the little pup had spunk. I also had to admit he was getting dangerously close to a tunnel. "Bubba," I warned.

"Shh," Bubba said, "I'm feeling more like a ghost. AROOOOOOO!"

Smack! Bubba ran into the side of a tunnel, head first. His eyes popped open and he rubbed his nose with a paw.

"Ha, ha, ha!" A laugh echoed through the yard.

"It's the ghost!" Floyd yelped.

WORSE THAN
A GHOST

After Floyd yelped, we all barked—every-one but Woodrow.

Woodrow waited for us to stop. "Calm down everybody," he said. "It's not a ghost. It's Tazz."

We looked up at the top of the wall. There sat the number-one neighborhood troublemaker.

"A cat!" Bubba said. "Isn't that worse than a ghost?"

Tazz perched on the top of the brick wall, slowly swishing her black-and-gold tail. The sun glinted off her eyes, making

them glow a spooky yellow color.

"Maybe it's not a cat at all," Floyd said with a whine. "Maybe it's a ghost that looks like a cat!"

Bubba jumped under my stomach and peered out from between my legs. "Are . . . are you a ghost?" he asked.

I was pretty sure Tazz was an ordinary cat. After all, she lived in the apartment across from mine, and I'd never seen her do a single ghostly thing. She didn't rattle chains. She never stomped across rooms. She didn't even say *BOO*. She did, however, tend to show up at the worst possible times and cause trouble. Believe me, I know. She'd gotten me into plenty of messes before.

"How long have you been up there?" Bubba asked Tazz.

"Long enough to know you'll never catch a ghost without my help," she purred.

43

"Do you know how to catch a ghost?" Bubba asked as he squeezed through my legs, almost tripping me. "Tell us! Please!"

"Hold on a dog-gone minute," I snapped. "We don't need Tazz. We were doing just fine before she came."

Woodrow, Blondie, and Floyd stared at me as if I'd just grown a banana for a tail. Bubba didn't stare. He spoke right up.

"We don't really know what to do," Bubba said. "Maybe we should see if Tazz has any ideas."

Tazz swished her bushy tail and purred even louder. "Smart words for a pup," she said.

Bubba put his front paws on the wall so he could get closer to Tazz. "What do we need to do to catch the ghost dog?" he asked.

Tazz stretched out on the top of the wall. "All you dogs need to do is think for yourselves, or should I say, smell for yourselves."

"Of course!" Woodrow shouted. "The cat is right! We can sniff out the ghost."

"What does a ghost smell like?" I asked.

Blondie daintily scratched behind her jeweled collar. "Maybe," she said, "you've been so busy looking you haven't really paid attention to any new scents in the yard."

"There's only one way to find out," Floyd said.

We lifted our noses high in the air and

sniffed. Even Woodrow, who usually lay on the ground half asleep, held his big nose high.

Barkley's School for Dogs was full of wonderful smells. There was the scent of trees, bushes, and dirt. There was the odor of Irish setter, dachshund, and retriever. I even recognized the ticklish smell of Tazz. But not a single sniff made me think ghost. We sniffed for a full twenty-nine seconds before Floyd gave up. "It's hopeless," he said.

"My nose is getting itchy," Blondie added.

"You're all hopeless," Tazz said. She shook her head and hopped off the other side of the wall.

I breathed in one last big breath. "Wait!" I shouted, my Wonder Dog nose high in the air. "I think I've got it."

No Way Out

My keen Wonder Dog sniffer kicked into high gear. I knew every smell there was to know. But just then, I definitely smelled something different.

With my nose to the ground I headed across the yard, determined to sniff every inch.

Blondie, Woodrow, Floyd, and Bubba sniffed with me for a while. "I don't smell anything new," Floyd said.

"All I smell is dog," Blondie added.

Bubba sniffed. "And trees," he said with a grin before he bounded over to a tree. He got distracted by a bush, and after that he raced for the teeter-totter to play. Pups are like that, so I let him go.

Woodrow yawned and headed for his pile of rags. "This old sniffer is too tired to help out anymore."

One by one they gave up. Not me. Wonder Dogs never give up. I stuck with it. I really did smell something new and the scent was definitely getting stronger.

The cold wind ruffled the hair of my bushy tail as I sniffed every tree, toy, and bush in Barkley's play yard.

The hair on the back of my neck stood up. The ghost dog was just behind that big bush. I could feel it. I took a deep breath and pushed through the thick branches. I could see why we hadn't found this hiding place before. It was a tangle of branches and almost impossible to wiggle through. Of course, nothing is impossible for a Wonder Dog.

"It's Jack, the Wonder Dog to the rescue!" I howled.

I did find something. It was white and furry, but it didn't look like a ghost to me. Instead, it looked like an ordinary short-haired dog that was more than a little bit dirty. I had been right all along. There are no such things as ghost dogs, and this little mutt proved it.

It looked like Woodrow had been right

about something else. Sweetcakes wasn't the culprit, after all, because her bone, Floyd's ball, Blondie's brush, my toy, and an empty bag of treats were under the bush, too. The white dog was almost my size and thumped his tail to be friendly.

"Hi!" he said with a little smile.

Never one to be rude, I barked hi back. Then I looked at the empty treat bag, and my tail stopped wagging faster than a flea can jump.

"Who are you?" I asked. "Why are you stealing our things?"

The dog lowered his head and stuck his tail between his legs. He looked up at me with sad brown eyes. "Sorry about that," he said, "but I was hungry and lonesome."

I had to admit this mutt looked a little on the sad side. It was hard to stay mad at him.

"Why didn't you come out and meet the rest of us?" I asked.

The dog peeked through the branches to make sure no one else had found his hiding place and whispered, "I don't belong here. I sneaked in."

I knew that to be impossible. It's a Fido Fact that Barkley's School for Dogs has a huge brick wall around it that no dog could climb. I told this dog the facts.

The dog nodded toward a big oak tree that grew on the outside of the wall. One big limb drooped down inside the wall. "I heard your barking and smelled the treats. I thought this would be a great place for a little rest. I used that tree to help me over. I can climb a tree almost as well as a cat, but once I got in here I was stuck. Like you said, there's no way out. I knew if the human found me he'd send me to the pound."

"Don't you have a home?" I asked.

The dog sighed. "I did. Once. I've lost my human. I've looked and looked for him. If the human here finds me and puts me in the pound, I may never see my home again."

I thought about my human, Maggie. I'd be more than sad if I lost her. I would never stop looking for her. Ever. I stared at the white dog with more than a little respect.

"I won't tell on you," I said. "Your secret is safe with me. In fact, Jack, the Wonder

Dog is going to help you!"

Then I told the white dog exactly what he had to do. "You must stay hidden until I figure out an escape plan."

"It's impossible," the white dog said with a whine. "There's no way out."

"Nothing is impossible," I told him. "But until I have a plan, don't move a hair on your head!"

10

Let a Lying Dog Lie

All that nosing around to find a ghost wore me to a frazzle. I fell in a heap beside Floyd and Blondie, ready to take a long nap, but not before I returned Floyd's ball.

"Where did you find it?" he asked.

I'm an honest dog. I refused to lie. I answered very carefully.

"Under a bush," I said, closing my eyes for a nap.

Floyd looked up from the ball for a minute. "I bet the ghost dog put it there. Did you find him?"

I opened one eye and looked into his big brown eyes. I couldn't lie, but I had promised the white dog I wouldn't let Fred find out about him. A Wonder Dog never breaks his promises, either. This was getting hard. Very hard.

"No ghost," I said wearily.

Blondie put her nose to my nose and asked, "Didn't you find anything?"

I opened my eye and stared into her beautiful eyes. This question was harder

to answer, but I was quick. "Sure," I admitted.

"I knew it!" Floyd yelled. "Where is that ghost dog? He's not going to get away with taking my ball."

I closed my eye again because I could not bear to look at Blondie. "I found lots of things," I said truthfully. "I found bugs and leaves and even a chipmunk." I peeked open one eye to see if Blondie and Floyd were buying my story. Blondie looked at me funny, as though she knew I was keeping something from her.

I shut my eyes tight, hoping they'd let me be. I pretended to nap. Well, actually I *did* nap. Searching for a ghost dog makes a hound tired.

When I woke up, I ate so much kibble my stomach nearly overflowed. I glanced around to make sure no one was watching. Blondie nibbled her lunch in tiny bites while Floyd and Woodrow gulped their food down in huge chunks. None of them paid any attention to me. I used the chance to load my jaws with as much kibble as I could carry.

My mouth was so full I could barely talk. I almost spit it all out when Blondie appeared beside me and asked, "What are you doing?"

"Nothing," I said, with little bits of kibble falling out from between my teeth.

Blondie looked at me with hurt eyes

and walked away. "Wait," I said, my mouth still full of kibble. But Blondie was already halfway across the yard.

I was almost to the secret hiding place when two huge paws blocked my way.

Sweetcakes stood in front of me like a prison warden, and she didn't look happy.

11

KiBBLE
DRiBBLE

If you've ever held food in your mouth for a long time, you know that it's enough to make you feel a little on the sick side. If Sweetcakes didn't get out of my way, she would end up with a face full of dog food.

"Where are you going?" Sweetcakes demanded.

Clyde came up beside us and growled, "Where? Where?"

I opened my mouth to answer, but the only thing that came out was a dribble of kibble.

"Hey, Sweetcakes," Blondie yelled from across the yard. "I think I found your bone." I wanted to hug Blondie for helping me out. She was a true friend. Sweetcakes took one last look at me and raced off with Clyde toward Blondie.

I took the chance to slip through the tangle of bushes and spit out my mouthful of food. The white dog met me with a smile. "Thanks," he said. "That's very nice of you."

The white dog didn't seem to mind that the food was slobbery. He sank his teeth into the kibble like it was a juicy steak. He stopped eating long enough to ask, "Did anyone follow you?"

The hair on my neck bristled. Follow me? Wasn't I Jack, the Wonder Dog? I shook my head no.

"You can't hide in here forever," I told the white dog. If Sweetcakes found out about him, she would blab everything to

Fred. The white dog would be kicked out on his little white ear. I strained my brain, trying to think of a way to get the white dog out of this mess.

That was when we heard the noise. The bushes rustled. My Wonder Dog ears picked it up right away. The white dog choked on kibble.

"I thought you said no one followed you," the white dog whined.

I shook my head. "No one did."

I knew Sweetcakes hadn't followed me, but maybe she'd figured out where I'd gone. She was mean enough to hunt me down just to cause trouble.

The white dog and I braced ourselves. There was no telling what Sweetcakes might do. But I wasn't prepared for what happened next.

FELINE FACT

It wasn't Sweetcakes who pushed through the bushes. It wasn't even a dog.

It was four dogs. All my friends had found us. I was relieved. "Thank goodness you're here," I said. Now I'd have some help.

"Are you the gh-gh-ghost dog?" Bubba asked the white dog. Blondie, Floyd, and even Woodrow crowded in behind Bubba. We were nose to nose in the tiny space.

I started to tell Bubba not to be silly, but the white dog answered first. "What makes you think I'm a ghost dog?"

66

"Fang-tastic, you are a ghost dog!" Floyd said. "I've never met a ghost dog before."

I stood there with my mouth hanging open, which is not a very pretty sight. Woodrow was a bit more sensible. "If you were a ghost, you wouldn't have to hide behind this bush," Woodrow said.

"Yeah," I said. "And a ghost wouldn't have any trouble getting out of here. Can't ghosts walk through walls?"

The white dog sniffed the brick wall and smiled, showing two long teeth. "Why, I bet you're right about that."

"I think we should get out of here before someone finds us," Blondie said, grabbing her brush.

I nodded. Fred would be bound to notice all of us missing from the yard before long. I looked at the white dog. "Don't worry, your secret is safe with us. We'll find a way to help you," I said.

The dog wagged his tail. "You already have."

Fred opened the back door and blew his whistle. We had to get back to training. After our lesson, I went back to the bush with a mouthful of water. I struggled under the bushes and couldn't believe what I saw. I was so surprised I spat water everywhere.

Nothing. The little dog was gone. All that was left was my toy, Sweetcakes's bone, and the empty treat bag. I sniffed around, but it was no use. The dog had disappeared.

I gathered the whole gang behind the bush. "Did someone help the white dog get away?" I asked.

"Not me," Woodrow, Bubba, and Floyd answered together.

"Me neither," Blondie sniffed.

"He couldn't have just disappeared," I said slowly.

"Unless," Bubba said, "he really *was* a ghost dog!"

"Looking for something?" A voice called from the wall above. It was Tazz. Her tail swished back and forth.

"What are you doing here?" I asked Tazz looking up at her.

"Oh, just doing a little ghost hunting," Tazz said, licking her paws.

"What do you know about ghosts?" Blondie asked.

Tazz swirled her tail over her nose. "Cats know a lot about ghosts. Like how to help them get out of difficult situations."

"I bet he was Rusty, the dog from the legend," Floyd whispered.

Woodrow yawned and shook his head. "I bet that dog found his way home all by himself."

"Or maybe he did disappear just like a ghost," Blondie said softly.

Or maybe the white dog had had a little help from Tazz. I looked up at Tazz just in time to see her wink.

ABOUT THE AUTHORS

Marcia Thornton Jones and Debbie Dadey used to work together at the same elementary school—Marcia taught in the classroom and Debbie was a librarian. But now they love writing about a totally different kind of school . . . where the students have four legs and a tail!

Marcia lives in Lexington, Kentucky, and Debbie lives in Fort Collins, Colorado. Their own pets have inspired them to write about Jack and his friends at Barkley's School. These authors have also written The Adventures of the Bailey School Kids, The Bailey City Monsters, and the Triplet Trouble series together.